THE EGO MACHINE

THE EGO MACHINE

by Henry Kuttner and C. L. Moore

When a slightly mad robot drunk on AC, wants you to join an experiment in optimum ecology—don't do it! After all, who wants to argue like Disraeli or live like Ivan the Terrible?

I

Nicholas Martin looked up at the robot across the desk.

"I'm not going to ask what you want," he said, in a low, restrained voice. "I already know. Just go away and tell St. Cyr I approve. Tell him I think it's wonderful, putting a robot in the picture. We've had everything else by now, except the Rockettes. But clearly a quiet little play about Christmas among the Portuguese fishermen on the Florida coast *must* have a robot. Only, why not six robots? Tell him I suggest a baker's dozen. Go away."

"Was your mother's name Helena Glinska?" the robot asked.

"It was not," Martin said.

"Ah, then she must have been the Great Hairy One," the robot murmured.

Martin took his feet off the desk and sat up slowly.

"It's quite all right," the robot said hastily. "You've been chosen for an ecological experiment, that's all. But it won't hurt. Robots are perfectly normal life forms where I come from, so you needn't—"

"Shut up," Martin said. "Robot indeed, you—you bit-player! This time St. Cyr has gone too far." He began to shake slightly all over, with some repressed but strong emotion. The intercom box on the desk caught his eye, and he stabbed a finger at one of the switches. "Get me Miss Ashby! Right away!"

"I'm so sorry," the robot said apologetically. "Have I made a mistake? The threshold fluctuations in the neurons always upset my mnemonic norm when I temporalize. Isn't this a crisis-point in your life?"

Martin breathed hard, which seemed to confirm the robot's assumption.

"Exactly," it said. "The ecological imbalance approaches a peak

5

that may destroy the life-form, unless ... mm-m. Now either you're about to be stepped on by a mammoth, locked in an iron mask, assassinated by helots, or—is this Sanskrit I'm speaking?" He shook his gleaming head. "Perhaps I should have got off fifty years ago, but I thought—sorry. Good-bye," he added hastily as Martin raised an angry glare.

Then the robot lifted a finger to each corner of his naturally rigid mouth, and moved his fingers horizontally in opposite directions, as though sketching an apologetic smile.

"No, don't go away," Martin said. "I want you right here, where the sight of you can refuel my rage in case it's needed. I wish to God I could get mad and stay mad," he added plaintively, gazing at the telephone.

"Are you sure your mother's name wasn't Helena Glinska?" the robot asked. It pinched thumb and forefinger together between its nominal brows, somehow giving the impression of a worried frown.

"Naturally I'm sure," Martin snapped.

"You aren't married yet, then? To Anastasia Zakharina-Koshkina?"

"Not yet or ever," Martin replied succinctly. The telephone rang. He snatched it up.

*

"Hello, Nick," said Erika Ashby's calm voice. "Something wrong?"

Instantly the fires of rage went out of Martin's eyes, to be replaced by a tender, rose-pink glow. For some years now he had given Erika, his very competent agent, ten percent of his take. He had also longed hopelessly to give her approximately a pound of flesh—the cardiac muscle, to put it in cold, unromantic terms. Martin did not; he put it in no terms at all, since whenever he tried to propose marriage to Erika he was taken with such fits of modesty that he could only babble o' green fields.

"Well," Erika repeated. "Something wrong?"

"Yes," Martin said, drawing a long breath. "Can St. Cyr make me marry somebody named Anastasia Zakharina-Koshkina?"

6

"What a wonderful memory you have," the robot put in mournfully. "Mine used to be, before I started temporalizing. But even radioactive neurons won't stand—"

"Nominally you're still entitled to life, liberty, et cetera," Erika said. "But I'm busy right now, Nick. Can't it wait till I see you?"

"When?"

"Didn't you get my message?" Erika demanded.

"Of course not," Martin said, angrily. "I've suspected for some time that all my incoming calls have to be cleared by St. Cyr. Somebody might try to smuggle in a word of hope, or possibly a file." His voice brightened. "Planning a jailbreak?"

"Oh, this is outrageous," Erika said. "Some day St. Cyr's going to go too far—"

"Not while he's got DeeDee behind him," Martin said gloomily. Summit Studios would sooner have made a film promoting atheism than offend their top box-office star, DeeDee Fleming. Even Tolliver Watt, who owned Summit lock, stock and barrel, spent wakeful nights because St. Cyr refused to let the lovely DeeDee sign a long-term contract.

"Nevertheless, Watt's no fool," Erika said. "I still think we could get him to give you a contract release if we could make him realize what a rotten investment you are. There isn't much time, though."

"Why not?"

"I told you—oh. Of course you don't know. He's leaving for Paris tomorrow morning."

Martin moaned. "Then I'm doomed," he said. "They'll pick up my option automatically next week and I'll never draw a free breath again. Erika, do something!"

"I'm going to," Erika said. "That's exactly what I want to see you about. Ah," she added suddenly, "now I understand why St. Cyr stopped my message. He was afraid. Nick, do you know what we've got to do?"

"See Watt?" Nick hazarded unhappily. "But Erika—"

"See Watt *alone*," Erika amplified.

"Not if St. Cyr can help it," Nick reminded her.

"Exactly. Naturally St. Cyr doesn't want us to talk to Watt privately. We might make him see reason. But this time, Nick, we've simply got to manage it somehow. One of us is going to talk to Watt while the other keeps St. Cyr at bay. Which do you choose?"

"Neither," Martin said promptly.

"Oh, Nick! I can't do the whole thing alone. Anybody'd think you were afraid of St. Cyr."

"I *am* afraid of St. Cyr," Martin said.

"Nonsense. What could he actually do to you?"

"He could terrorize me. He does it all the time. Erika, he says I'm indoctrinating beautifully. Doesn't it make your blood run cold? Look at all the other writers he's indoctrinated."

"I know. I saw one of them on Main Street last week, delving into garbage cans. Do you want to end up that way? Then stand up for your rights!"

"Ah," said the robot wisely, nodding. "Just as I thought. A crisis-point."

"Shut up," Martin said. "No, not you, Erika. I'm sorry."

"So am I," Erika said tartly. "For a moment I thought you'd acquired a backbone."

"If I were somebody like Hemingway—" Martin began in a miserable voice.

"Did you say Hemingway?" the robot inquired. "Is this the Kinsey-Hemingway era? Then I must be right. You're Nicholas Martin, the next subject. Martin, Martin? Let me see—oh yes, the Disraeli type, that's it." He rubbed his forehead with a grating sound. "Oh, my poor neuron thresholds! Now I remember."

*

"Nick, can you hear me?" Erika's voice inquired. "I'm coming over there right away. Brace yourself. We're going to beard St. Cyr in his den and convince Watt you'll never make a good screen-writer. Now—"

"But St. Cyr won't *ever* admit that," Martin cried. "He doesn't know the meaning of the word failure. He says so. He's going to make me into a screen-writer or kill me."

"Remember what happened to Ed Cassidy?" Erika reminded him grimly. "St. Cyr didn't make him into a screen-writer."

"True. Poor old Ed," Martin said, with a shiver.

"All right, then. I'm on my way. Anything else?"

"Yes!" Martin cried, drawing a deep breath. "Yes, there is! I love you madly!"

But the words never got past his glottis. Opening and closing his mouth noiselessly, the cowardly playwright finally clenched his teeth and tried again. A faint, hopeless squeak vibrated the telephone's disk. Martin let his shoulders slump hopelessly. It was clear he could never propose to anybody, not even a harmless telephone.

"Did you say something?" Erika asked. "Well, good-bye then."

"Wait a minute," Martin said, his eyes suddenly falling once more upon the robot. Speechless on one subject only, he went on rapidly, "I forgot to tell you. Watt and the nest-fouling St. Cyr have just hired a mock-up phony robot to play in *Angelina Noel*!"

But the line was dead.

"I'm not a phony," the robot said, hurt.

Martin fell back in his chair and stared at his guest with dull, hopeless eyes. "Neither was King Kong," he remarked. "Don't start feeding me some line St. Cyr's told you to pull. I know he's trying to break my nerve. He'll probably do it, too. Look what he's done to my play already. Why Fred Waring? I don't mind Fred Waring in his proper place. There he's fine. But not in *Angelina Noel*. Not as the Portuguese captain of a fishing boat manned by his entire band, accompanied by Dan Dailey singing *Napoli* to DeeDee Fleming in a mermaid's tail—"

Self-stunned by this recapitulation, Martin put his arms on the desk, his head in his hands, and to his horror found himself giggling. The telephone rang. Martin groped for the instrument without rising from his semi-recumbent position.

"Who?" he asked shakily. "*Who?* St. Cyr—"

A hoarse bellow came over the wire. Martin sat bolt upright, seizing the phone desperately with both hands.

"Listen!" he cried. "Will you let me finish what I'm going to say, just for once? Putting a robot in *Angelina Noel* is simply—"

"I do not hear what you say," roared a heavy voice. "Your idea stinks. Whatever it is. Be at Theater One for yesterday's rushes! At once!"

"But wait—"

St. Cyr belched and hung up. Martin's strangling hands tightened briefly on the telephone. But it was no use. The real strangle-hold was the one St. Cyr had around Martin's throat, and it had been tightening now for nearly thirteen weeks. Or had it been thirteen years? Looking backward, Martin could scarcely believe that only a short time ago he had been a free man, a successful Broadway playwright, the author of the hit play *Angelina Noel*. Then had come St. Cyr....

A snob at heart, the director loved getting his clutches on hit plays and name writers. Summit Studios, he had roared at Martin, would follow the original play exactly and would give Martin the final okay on the script, provided he signed a thirteen-week contract to help write the screen treatment. This had seemed too good to be true—and was.

Martin's downfall lay partly in the fine print and partly in the fact that Erika Ashby had been in the hospital with a bad attack of influenza at the time. Buried in legal verbiage was a clause that bound Martin to five years of servitude with Summit should they pick up his option. Next week they would certainly do just that, unless justice prevailed.

*

"I think I need a drink," Martin said unsteadily. "Or several." He glanced toward the robot. "I wonder if you'd mind getting me that bottle of Scotch from the bar over there."

"But I am here to conduct an experiment in optimum ecology," said the robot.

Martin closed his eyes. "Pour me a drink," he pleaded. "Please. Then put the glass in my hand, will you? It's not much to ask. After all, we're both human beings, aren't we?"

"Well, no," the robot said, placing a brimming glass in Martin's groping fingers. Martin drank. Then he opened his eyes and blinked at the tall highball glass in his hand. The robot had filled it to the brim with Scotch. Martin turned a wondering gaze on his metallic companion.

"You must do a lot of drinking yourself," he said thoughtfully. "I suppose tolerance can be built up. Go ahead. Help yourself. Take the rest of the bottle."

The robot placed the tip of a finger above each eye and slid the fingers upward, as though raising his eyebrows inquiringly.

"Go on, have a jolt," Martin urged. "Or don't you want to break bread with me, under the circumstances?"

"How can I?" the robot asked. "I'm a robot." His voice sounded somewhat wistful. "What happens?" he inquired. "Is it a lubricatory or a fueling mechanism?"

Martin glanced at his brimming glass.

"Fueling," he said tersely. "High octane. You really believe in staying in character, don't you? Why not—"

"Oh, the principle of irritation," the robot interrupted. "I see. Just like fermented mammoth's milk."

Martin choked. "Have you ever drunk fermented mammoth's milk?" he inquired.

"How could I?" the robot asked. "But I've seen it done." He drew a straight line vertically upward between his invisible eyebrows, managing to look wistful. "Of course my world is perfectly functional and functionally perfect, but I can't help finding temporalizing a fascina—" He broke off. "I'm wasting space-time. Ah. Now. Mr. Martin, would you be willing to—"

"Oh, have a drink," Martin said. "I feel hospitable. Go ahead, indulge me, will you? My pleasures are few. And I've got to go and be terrorized in a minute, anyhow. If you can't get that mask off I'll send for a straw. You can step out of character long enough for one jolt, can't you?"

"I'd like to try it," the robot said pensively. "Ever since I noticed the effect fermented mammoth's milk had on the boys, it's been on my mind, rather. Quite easy for a human, of course. Technically it's simple enough, I see now. The irritation just increases the frequency of the brain's kappa waves, as with boosted voltage, but since electrical voltage never existed in pre-robot times—"

"It did," Martin said, taking another drink. "I mean, it does. What do you call that, a mammoth?" He indicated the desk lamp.

The robot's jaw dropped.

"That?" he asked in blank amazement. "Why—why then all those telephone poles and dynamos and lighting-equipment I noticed in this era are powered by electricity!"

"What did you think they were powered by?" Martin asked coldly.

"Slaves," the robot said, examining the lamp. He switched it on, blinked, and then unscrewed the bulb. "Voltage, you say?"

"Don't be a fool," Martin said. "You're overplaying your part. I've got to get going in a minute. Do you want a jolt or don't you?"

"Well," the robot said, "I don't want to seem unsociable. This *ought* to work." So saying, he stuck his finger in the lamp-socket. There was a brief, crackling flash. The robot withdrew his finger.

"$F(t)$—" he said, and swayed slightly. Then his fingers came up and sketched a smile that seemed, somehow, to express delighted surprise.

"$Fff(t)$!" he said, and went on rather thickly, "$F(t)$ integral between plus and minus infinity ... a-sub-n to e...."

Martin's eyes opened wide with shocked horror. Whether a doctor or a psychiatrist should be called in was debatable, but it was perfectly evident that this was a case for the medical profession, and the sooner the better. Perhaps the police, too. The bit-player in the robot suit was clearly as mad as a hatter. Martin poised indecisively, waiting for his lunatic guest either to drop dead or spring at his throat.

The robot appeared to be smacking his lips, with faint clicking sounds.

"Why, that's wonderful," he said. "AC, too."

"Y-you're not dead?" Martin inquired shakily.

"I'm not even alive," the robot murmured. "The way you'd understand it, that is. Ah—thanks for the jolt."

*

Martin stared at the robot with the wildest dawning of surmise.

"Why—" he gasped. "Why—*you're a robot!*"

"Certainly I'm a robot," his guest said. "What slow minds you pre-robots had. Mine's working like lightning now." He stole a drunkard's glance at the desk-lamp. "$F(t)$—I mean, if you counted the kappa waves of my radio-atomic brain now, you'd be amazed how the frequency's increased." He paused thoughtfully. "$F(t)$," he added.

Moving quite slowly, like a man under water, Martin lifted his glass and drank whiskey. Then, cautiously, he looked up at the robot again.

"$F(t)$—" he said, paused, shuddered, and drank again. That did it. "I'm drunk," he said with an air of shaken relief. "That must be it. I was almost beginning to believe—'

"Oh, nobody believes I'm a robot at first," the robot said. "You'll notice I showed up in a movie lot, where I wouldn't arouse suspicion. I'll appear to Ivan Vasilovich in an alchemist's lab, and he'll jump to the conclusive I'm an automaton. Which, of course, I *am*. Then there's a Uighur on my list—I'll appear to him in a shaman's hut and he'll assume I'm a devil. A matter of ecologicologic."

"Then you're a devil?" Martin inquired, seizing on the only plausible solution.

13

"No, no, no. I'm a robot. Don't you understand anything?"

"I don't even know who I am, now," Martin said. "For all I know, I'm a faun and you're a human child. I don't think this Scotch is doing me as much good as I'd—"

"Your name is Nicholas Martin," the robot said patiently. "And mine is ENIAC."

"Eniac?"

"ENIAC," the robot corrected, capitalizing. "ENIAC Gamma the Ninety-Third."

So saying, he unslung a sack from his metallic shoulder and began to rummage out length upon length of what looked like red silk ribbon with a curious metallic lustre. After approximately a quarter-mile of it had appeared, a crystal football helmet emerged attached to its end. A gleaming red-green stone was set on each side of the helmet.

"Just over the temporal lobes, you see," the robot explained, indicating the jewels. "Now you just set it on your head, like this—"

"Oh no I don't," Martin said, withdrawing his head with the utmost rapidity. "Neither do you, my friend. What's the idea? I don't like the looks of that gimmick. I particularly don't like those two red garnets on the sides. They look like eyes."

"Those are artificial eclogite," the robot assured him. "They simply have a high dielectric constant. It's merely a matter of altering the normal thresholds of the neuron memory-circuits. All thinking is based on memory, you know. The strength of your associations—the emotional indices of your memories—channel your actions and decisions, and the ecologizer simply changes the voltage of your brain so the thresholds are altered."

"Is that all it does?" Martin asked suspiciously.

"Well, now," the robot said with a slight air of evasion. "I didn't intend to mention it, but since you ask—it also imposes the master-matrix of your character type. But since that's the prototype of your character in the first place, it will simply enable you to make the most of your potential ability, hereditary and acquired. It will make you react to your environment in the way that best assures your survival."

"Not me, it won't," Martin said firmly. "Because you aren't going to put that thing on my head."

The robot sketched a puzzled frown. "Oh," he said after a pause. "I haven't explained yet, have I? It's very simple. Would you be willing to take part in a valuable socio-cultural experiment for the benefit of all mankind?"

"No," Martin said.

"But you don't know what it is yet," the robot said plaintively. "You'll be the only one to refuse, after I've explained everything thoroughly. By the way, can you understand me all right?"

Martin laughed hollowly. "Natch," he said.

"Good," the robot said, relieved. "That may be one trouble with my memory. I had to record so many languages before I could temporalize. Sanskrit's very simple, but medieval Russian's confusing, and as for Uighur—however! The purpose of this experiment is to promote the most successful pro-survival relationship between man and his environment. Instant adaptation is what we're aiming at, and we hope to get it by minimizing the differential between individual and environment. In other words, the right reaction at the right time. Understand?"

"Of course not," Martin said. "What nonsense you talk."

"There are," the robot said rather wearily, "only a limited number of character matrices possible, depending first on the arrangement of the genes within the chromosomes, and later upon environmental additions. Since environments tend to repeat—like societies, you know—an organizational pattern isn't hard to lay out, along the Kaldekooz time-scale. You follow me so far?"

"By the Kaldekooz time-scale, yes," Martin said.

"I was always lucid," the robot remarked a little vainly, nourishing a swirl of red ribbon.

"Keep that thing away from me," Martin complained. "Drunk I may be, but I have no intention of sticking my neck out that far."

"Of course you'll do it," the robot said firmly. "Nobody's ever refused yet. And don't bicker with me or you'll get me confused and I'll have to take another jolt of voltage. Then there's no telling how confused I'll be. My memory gives me enough trouble when I temporalize. Time-travel always raises the synaptic delay threshold, but the trouble is it's so variable. That's why I got you mixed up with Ivan at first. But I don't visit him till after I've seen you—I'm running the test chronologically, and nineteen-fifty-two comes before fifteen-seventy, of course."

"It doesn't," Martin said, tilting the glass to his lips. "Not even in Hollywood does nineteen-fifty-two come before fifteen-seventy."

"I'm using the Kaldekooz time-scale," the robot explained. "But really only for convenience. Now do you want the ideal ecological differential or don't you? Because—" Here he flourished the red ribbon again, peered into the helmet, looked narrowly at Martin, and shook his head.

"I'm sorry," the robot said. "I'm afraid this won't work. Your head's too small. Not enough brain-room, I suppose. This helmet's for an eight and a half head, and yours is much too—"

"My head *is* eight and a half," Martin protested with dignity.

"Can't be," the robot said cunningly. "If it were, the helmet would fit, and it doesn't. Too big."

"It does fit," Martin said.

"That's the trouble with arguing with pre-robot species," ENIAC said, as to himself. "Low, brutish, unreasoning. No wonder, when their heads are so small. Now Mr. Martin—" He spoke as though to a small, stupid, stubborn child. "Try to understand. This helmet's size eight and a half. Your head is unfortunately so very small that the helmet wouldn't fit—"

"Blast it!" cried the infuriated Martin, caution quite lost between Scotch and annoyance. "It does fit! Look here!" Recklessly he snatched the helmet and clapped it firmly on his head. "It fits perfectly!"

"I erred," the robot acknowledged, with such a gleam in his eye that Martin, suddenly conscious of his rashness, jerked the helmet from his head and dropped it on the desk. ENIAC quietly picked it up and put it back into his sack, stuffing the red ribbon in after it with rapid motions. Martin watched, baffled, until ENIAC had finished, gathered together the mouth of the sack, swung it on his shoulder again, and turned toward the door.

"Good-bye," the robot said. "And thank you."

"For what?" Martin demanded.

"For your cooperation," the robot said.

"I won't cooperate," Martin told him flatly. "It's no use. Whatever fool treatment it is you're selling, I'm not going to—"

"Oh, you've already had the ecology treatment," ENIAC replied blandly. "I'll be back tonight to renew the charge. It lasts only twelve hours."

"*What!*"

ENIAC moved his forefingers outward from the corners of his mouth, sketching a polite smile. Then he stepped through the door and closed it behind him.

Martin made a faint squealing sound, like a stuck but gagged pig. *Something was happening inside his head.*

II

Nicholas Martin felt like a man suddenly thrust under an ice-cold shower. No, not cold—steaming hot. Perfumed, too. The wind that blew in from the open window bore with it a frightful stench of gasoline, sagebrush, paint, and—from the distant commissary—ham sandwiches.

"Drunk," he thought frantically. "I'm drunk—or crazy!" He sprang up and spun around wildly; then catching sight of a crack in the hardwood floor he tried to walk along it. "Because if I can walk a straight line," he thought, "I'm not drunk. I'm only crazy...." It was not a very comforting thought.

He could walk it, all right. He could walk a far straighter line than the crack, which he saw now was microscopically jagged. He had, in fact, never felt such a sense of location and equilibrium in his life. His experiment carried him across the room to a wall-mirror, and as he straightened to look into it, suddenly all confusion settled and ceased. The violent sensory perceptions leveled off and returned to normal.

Everything was quiet. Everything was all right.

Martin met his own eyes in the mirror.

Everything was *not* all right.

He was stone cold sober. The Scotch he had drunk might as well have been spring-water. He leaned closer to the mirror, trying to stare through his own eyes into the depths of his brain. For something extremely odd was happening in there. All over his brain, tiny shutters were beginning to move, some sliding up till only a narrow crack remained, through which the beady little eyes of neurons could be seen peeping, some sliding down with faint crashes, revealing the agile, spidery forms of still other neurons scuttling for cover.

Altered thresholds, changing the yes-and-no reaction time of the memory-circuits, with their key emotional indices and associations ... huh?

The robot!

Martin's head swung toward the closed office door. But he made no further move. The look of blank panic on his face very slowly, quite unconsciously, began to change. The robot ... could wait.

Automatically Martin raised his hand, as though to adjust an invisible monocle. Behind him, the telephone began to ring. Martin glanced at it.

His lips curved into an insolent smile.

Flicking dust from his lapel with a suave gesture, Martin picked up the telephone. He said nothing. There was a long silence. Then a hoarse voice shouted, "Hello, hello, hello! Are you there? You, Martin!"

Martin said absolutely nothing at all.

"You keep me waiting," the voice bellowed. "Me, St. Cyr! Now jump! The rushes are ... Martin, do you hear me?"

Martin gently laid down the receiver on the desk. He turned again toward the mirror, regarded himself critically, frowned.

"Dreary," he murmured. "Distinctly dreary. I wonder why I ever bought this necktie?"

The softly bellowing telephone distracted him. He studied the instrument briefly, then clapped his hands sharply together an inch from the mouthpiece. There was a sharp, anguished cry from the other end of the line.

"Very good," Martin murmured, turning away. "That robot has done me a considerable favor. I should have realized the possibilities sooner. After all, a super-machine, such as ENIAC, would be far cleverer than a man, who is merely an ordinary machine. Yes," he added, stepping into the hall and coming face to face with Toni LaMotta, who was currently working for Summit on loan. "'*Man is a machine, and woman—*'" Here he gave Miss LaMotta a look of such arrogant significance that she was quite startled.

"'*And woman—a toy*,'" Martin amplified, as he turned toward Theater One, where St. Cyr and destiny awaited him.

*

Summit Studios, outdoing even MGM, always shot ten times as much footage as necessary on every scene. At the beginning of each shooting day, this confusing mass of celluloid was shown in St. Cyr's private projection theater, a small but luxurious domed room furnished with lie-back chairs and every other convenience, though no screen was visible until you looked up. Then you saw it on the ceiling.

When Martin entered, it was instantly evident that ecology took a sudden shift toward the worse. Operating on the theory that the old

19

Nicholas Martin had come into it, the theater, which had breathed an expensive air of luxurious confidence, chilled toward him. The nap of the Persian rug shrank from his contaminating feet. The chair he stumbled against in the half-light seemed to shrug contemptuously. And the three people in the theater gave him such a look as might be turned upon one of the larger apes who had, by sheer accident, got an invitation to Buckingham Palace.

DeeDee Fleming (her real name was impossible to remember, besides having not a vowel in it) lay placidly in her chair, her feet comfortably up, her lovely hands folded, her large, liquid gaze fixed upon the screen where DeeDee Fleming, in the silvery meshes of a technicolor mermaid, swam phlegmatically through seas of pearl-colored mist.

Martin groped in the gloom for a chair. The strangest things were going on inside his brain, where tiny stiles still moved and readjusted until he no longer felt in the least like Nicholas Martin. Who did he feel like, then? What had happened?

He recalled the neurons whose beady little eyes he had fancied he saw staring brightly into, as well as out of, his own. Or had he? The memory was vivid, yet it couldn't be, of course. The answer was perfectly simple and terribly logical. ENIAC Gamma the Ninety-Third had told him, somewhat ambiguously, just what his ecological experiment involved. Martin had merely been given the optimum reactive pattern of his successful prototype, a man who had most thoroughly controlled his own environment. And ENIAC had told him the man's name, along with several confusing references to other prototypes like an Ivan (who?) and an unnamed Uighur.

The name for Martin's prototype was, of course, Disraeli, Earl of Beaconsfield. Martin had a vivid recollection of George Arliss playing the role. Clever, insolent, eccentric in dress and manner, exuberant, suave, self-controlled, with a strongly perceptive imagination....

"No, no, no!" DeeDee said with a sort of calm impatience. "Be careful, Nick. Some other chair, please. I have my feet on this one."

"T-t-t-t-t," said Raoul St. Cyr, protruding his thick lips and snapping the fingers of an enormous hand as he pointed to a lowly chair against the wall. "Behind me, Martin. Sit down, sit down. Out of our way. Now! Pay attention. Study what I have done to make something great out of your foolish little play. Especially note how I have so cleverly ended the solo by building to five cumulative pratt-falls. Timing is all," he finished. "Now—SILENCE!"

For a man born in the obscure little Balkan country of Mixo-Lydia, Raoul St. Cyr had done very well for himself in Hollywood. In 1939 St. Cyr, growing alarmed at the imminence of war, departed for America, taking with him the print of an unpronounceable Mixo-Lydian film he had made, which might be translated roughly as *The Pores In the Face of the Peasant.*

With this he established his artistic reputation as a great director, though if the truth were known, it was really poverty that caused *The Pores* to be so artistically lighted, and simple drunkenness which had made most of the cast act out one of the strangest performances in film history. But critics compared *The Pores* to a ballet and praised inordinately the beauty of its leading lady, now known to the world as DeeDee Fleming.

DeeDee was so incredibly beautiful that the law of compensation would force one to expect incredible stupidity as well. One was not disappointed. DeeDee's neurons didn't know *anything.* She had heard of emotions, and under St. Cyr's bullying could imitate a few of them, but other directors had gone mad trying to get through the semantic block that kept DeeDee's mind a calm, unruffled pool possibly three inches deep. St. Cyr merely bellowed. This simple, primordial approach seemed to be the only one that made sense to Summit's greatest investment and top star.

With this whip-hand over the beautiful and brainless DeeDee, St. Cyr quickly rose to the top in Hollywood. He had undoubted talent. He could make one picture very well indeed. He had made it twenty times already, each time starring DeeDee, and each time perfecting his own feudalistic production unit. Whenever anyone disagreed with St. Cyr, he had only to threaten to go over to MGM and take the obedient DeeDee with him, for he had never allowed her to sign a long-term contract and she worked only on a picture-to-picture basis. Even Tolliver Watt knuckled under when St. Cyr voiced the threat of removing DeeDee.

*

"Sit down, Martin," Tolliver Watt said. He was a tall, lean, hatchet-faced man who looked like a horse being starved because he was too proud to eat hay. With calm, detached omnipotence he inclined his grey-shot head a millimeter, while a faintly pained expression passed fleetingly across his face.

"Highball, please," he said.

A white-clad waiter appeared noiselessly from nowhere and glided forward with a tray. It was at this point that Martin felt the last stiles readjust in his brain, and entirely on impulse he reached out and took the frosted highball glass from the tray. Without observing this the waiter glided on and presented Watt with a gleaming salver full of nothing. Watt and the waiter regarded the tray.

Then their eyes met. There was a brief silence.

"Here," Martin said, replacing the glass. "Much too weak. Get me another, please. I'm reorienting toward a new phase, which means a different optimum," he explained to the puzzled Watt as he readjusted a chair beside the great man and dropped into it. Odd that he had never before felt at ease during rushes. Right now he felt fine. Perfectly at ease. Relaxed.

"Scotch and soda for Mr. Martin," Watt said calmly. "And another for me."

"So, so, so, now we begin," St. Cyr cried impatiently. He spoke into a hand microphone. Instantly the screen on the ceiling flickered noisily and began to unfold a series of rather ragged scenes in which a chorus of mermaids danced on their tails down the street of a little

Florida fishing village.

To understand the full loathsomeness of the fate facing Nicholas Martin, it is necessary to view a St. Cyr production. It seemed to Martin that he was watching the most noisome movie ever put upon film. He was conscious that St. Cyr and Watt were stealing rather mystified glances at him. In the dark he put up two fingers and sketched a robot-like grin. Then, feeling sublimely sure of himself, he lit a cigarette and chuckled aloud.

"You laugh?" St. Cyr demanded with instant displeasure. "You do not appreciate great art? What do you know about it, eh? Are you a genius?"

"This," Martin said urbanely, "is the most noisome movie ever put on film."

In the sudden, deathly quiet which followed, Martin flicked ashes elegantly and added, "With my help, you may yet avoid becoming the laughing stock of the whole continent. Every foot of this picture must be junked. Tomorrow bright and early we will start all over, and—"

Watt said quietly, "We're quite competent to make a film out of *Angelina Noel*, Martin."

"It is artistic!" St. Cyr shouted. "And it will make money, too!"

"Bah, money!" Martin said cunningly. He flicked more ash with a lavish gesture. "Who cares about money? Let Summit worry."

Watt leaned forward to peer searchingly at Martin in the dimness.

"Raoul," he said, glancing at St. Cyr, "I understood you were getting your—ah—your new writers whipped into shape. This doesn't sound to me as if—"

"Yes, yes, yes, yes," St. Cyr cried excitedly. "Whipped into shape, exactly! A brief delirium, eh? Martin, you feel well? You feel yourself?"

Martin laughed with quiet confidence. "Never fear," he said. "The money you spend on me is well worth what I'll bring you in prestige. I quite understand. Our confidential talks were not to be secret from

Watt, of course."

"What confidential talks?" bellowed St. Cyr thickly, growing red.

"We need keep nothing from Watt, need we?" Martin went on imperturably. "You hired me for prestige, and prestige you'll get, if you can only keep your big mouth shut long enough. I'll make the name of St. Cyr glorious for you. Naturally you may lose something at the box-office, but it's well worth—"

"*Pjrzqxgl!*" roared St. Cyr in his native tongue, and he lumbered up from the chair, brandishing the microphone in an enormous, hairy hand.

Deftly Martin reached out and twitched it from his grasp.

"Stop the film," he ordered crisply.

It was very strange. A distant part of his mind knew that normally he would never have dared behave this way, but he felt convinced that never before in his life had he acted with complete normality. He glowed with a giddy warmth of confidence that everything he did would be right, at least while the twelve-hour treatment lasted....

*

The screen flickered hesitantly, then went blank.

"Turn the lights on," Martin ordered the unseen presence beyond the mike. Softly and suddenly the room glowed with illumination. And upon the visages of Watt and St. Cyr he saw a mutual dawning uneasiness begin to break.

He had just given them food for thought. But he had given them more than that. He tried to imagine what moved in the minds of the two men, below the suspicions he had just implanted. St. Cyr's was fairly obvious. The Mixo-Lydian licked his lips—no mean task—and studied Martin with uneasy little bloodshot eyes. Clearly Martin had acquired confidence from somewhere. What did it mean? What secret sin of St. Cyr's had been discovered to him, what flaw in his contract, that he dared behave so defiantly?

Tolliver Watt was a horse of another color; apparently the man had no guilty secrets; but he too looked uneasy. Martin studied the proud face and probed for inner weaknesses. Watt would be a harder nut to crack. But Martin could do it.

"That last underwater sequence," he now said, pursuing his theme. "Pure trash, you know. It'll have to come out. The whole scene must be shot from under water."

"Shut up!" St. Cyr shouted violently.

"But it must, you know," Martin went on. "Or it won't jibe with the new stuff I've written in. In fact, I'm not at all certain that the whole picture shouldn't be shot under water. You know, we could use the documentary technique—"

"Raoul," Watt said suddenly, "what's this man trying to do?"

"He is trying to break his contract, of course," St. Cyr said, turning ruddy olive. "It is the bad phase all my writers go through before I get them whipped into shape. In Mixo-Lydia—"

"Are you sure he'll whip into shape?" Watt asked.

"To me this is now a personal matter," St. Cyr said, glaring at Martin. "I have spent nearly thirteen weeks on this man and I do not intend to waste my valuable time on another. I tell you he is simply trying to break his contract—tricks, tricks, tricks."

"Are you?" Watt asked Martin coldly.

"Not now," Martin said. "I've changed my mind. My agent insists I'd be better off away from Summit. In fact, she has the curious feeling that I and Summit would suffer by a mesalliance. But for the first time I'm not sure I agree. I begin to see possibilities, even in the tripe St. Cyr has been stuffing down the public's throat for years. Of course I can't work miracles all at once. Audiences have come to expect garbage from Summit, and they've even been conditioned to like it. But we'll begin in a small way to re-educate them with this picture. I suggest we try to symbolize the Existentialist hopelessness of it all by ending the film with a full four hundred feet of seascapes—nothing but vast, heaving stretches of ocean," he ended, on a note of complacent satisfaction.

A vast, heaving stretch of Raoul St. Cyr rose from his chair and advanced upon Martin.

"Outside, outside!" he shouted. "Back to your cell, you double-crossing vermin! I, Raoul St. Cyr, command it. Outside, before I rip you limb from limb—"

Martin spoke quickly. His voice was calm, but he knew he would have to work fast.

"You see, Watt?" he said clearly, meeting Watt's rather startled gaze. "Doesn't dare let you exchange three words with me, for fear I'll let something slip. No wonder he's trying to put me out of here—he's skating on thin ice these days."

Goaded, St. Cyr rolled forward in a ponderous lunge, but Watt interposed. It was true, of course, that the writer was probably trying to break his contract. But there were wheels within wheels here. Martin was too confident, too debonaire. Something was going on which Watt did not understand.

"All right, Raoul," he said decisively. "Relax for a minute. I said relax! We don't want Nick here suing you for assault and battery, do we? Your artistic temperament carries you away sometimes. Relax and let's hear what Nick has to say."

"Watch out for him, Tolliver!" St. Cyr cried warningly. "They're cunning, these creatures. Cunning as rats. You never know—"

Martin raised the microphone with a lordly gesture. Ignoring the director, he said commandingly into the mike, "Put me through to the commissary. The bar, please. Yes. I want to order a drink. Something very special. A—ah—a Helena Glinska—"

*

"Hello," Erika Ashby's voice said from the door. "Nick, are you there? May I come in?"

The sound of her voice sent delicious chills rushing up and down Martin's spine. He swung round, mike in hand, to welcome her. But St. Cyr, pleased at this diversion, roared before he could speak.

"No, no, no, no! Go! Go at once. Whoever you are—*out!*"

Erika, looking very brisk, attractive and firm, marched into the room and cast at Martin a look of resigned patience.

Very clearly she expected to fight both her own battles and his.

"I'm on business here," she told St. Cyr coldly. "You can't part author and agent like this. Nick and I want to have a word with Mr. Watt."

"Ah, my pretty creature, sit down," Martin said in a loud, clear voice, scrambling out of his chair. "Welcome! I'm just ordering myself a drink. Will you have something?"

Erika looked at him with startled suspicion. "No, and neither will you," she said. "How many have you had already? Nick, if you're drunk at a time like this—"

"And no shilly-shallying," Martin said blandly into the mike. "I want it at once, do you hear? A Helena Glinska, yes. Perhaps you don't know it? Then listen carefully. Take the largest Napoleon you've got. If you haven't a big one, a small punch bowl will do. Fill it half full with ice-cold ale. Got that? Add three jiggers of creme de menthe—"

"Nick, are you mad?" Erika demanded, revolted.

"—and six jiggers of honey," Martin went on placidly. "Stir, don't shake. Never shake a Helena Glinska. Keep it well chilled, and—"

"Miss Ashby, we are very busy," St. Cyr broke in importantly, making shooing motions toward the door. "Not now. Sorry. You interrupt. Go at once."

"—better add six more jiggers of honey," Martin was heard to add contemplatively into the mike. "And then send it over immediately. Drop everything else, and get it here within sixty seconds. There's a bonus for you if you do. Okay? Good. See to it."

He tossed the microphone casually at St. Cyr.

Meanwhile, Erika had closed in on Tolliver Watt.

"I've just come from talking to Gloria Eden," she said, "and she's willing to do a one-picture deal with Summit *if* I okay it. But I'm not going to okay it unless you release Nick Martin from his contract, and that's flat."

Watt showed pleased surprise.

"Well, we might get together on that," he said instantly, for he was a fan of Miss Eden's and for a long time had yearned to star her in a remake of *Vanity Fair*. "Why didn't you bring her along? We could have—"

"Nonsense!" St. Cyr shouted. "Do not discuss this matter yet, Tolliver."

"She's down at Laguna," Erika explained. "Be quiet, St. Cyr! I won't—"

A knock at the door interrupted her. Martin hurried to open it and as he had expected encountered a waiter with a tray.

"Quick work," he said urbanely, accepting the huge, coldly sweating Napoleon in a bank of ice. "Beautiful, isn't it?"

St. Cyr's booming shouts from behind him drowned out whatever remark the waiter may have made as he received a bill from Martin and withdrew, looking nauseated.

"No, no, no, no," St. Cyr was roaring. "Tolliver, we can get Gloria and keep this writer too, not that he is any good, but I have spent already thirteen weeks training him in the St. Cyr approach. Leave it to me. In Mixo-Lydia we handle—"

Erika's attractive mouth was opening and shutting, her voice unheard in the uproar. St. Cyr could keep it up indefinitely, as was well known in Hollywood. Martin sighed, lifted the brimming Napoleon and sniffed delicately as he stepped backward toward his chair. When his heel touched it, he tripped with the utmost grace and savoir-faire, and very deftly emptied the Helena Glinsak, ale, honey, creme de menthe, ice and all, over St. Cyr's capacious front.

St. Cyr's bellow broke the microphone.

*

Martin had composed his invention carefully. The nauseous brew combined the maximum elements of wetness, coldness, stickiness and pungency.

The drenched St. Cyr, shuddering violently as the icy beverage deluged his legs, snatched out his handkerchief and mopped in vain. The handkerchief merely stuck to his trousers, glued there by twelve jiggers of honey. He reeked of peppermint.

"I suggest we adjourn to the commissary," Martin said fastidiously. "In some private booth we can go on with this discussion away from the—the rather overpowering smell of peppermint."

"In Mixo-Lydia," St. Cyr gasped, sloshing in his shoes as he turned toward Martin, "in Mixo-Lydia we throw to the dogs—we boil in oil—we—"

"And next time," Martin said, "please don't joggle my elbow when I'm holding a Helena Glinska. It's most annoying."

St. Cyr drew a mighty breath, rose to his full height—and then subsided. St. Cyr at the moment looked like a Keystone Kop after the chase sequence, and knew it. Even if he killed Martin now, the element of classic tragedy would be lacking. He would appear in the untenable position of Hamlet murdering his uncle with custard pies.

"Do nothing until I return!" he commanded, and with a final glare at Martin plunged moistly out of the theater.

The door crashed shut behind him. There was silence for a moment except for the soft music from the overhead screen which DeeDee had caused to be turned on again, so that she might watch her own lovely form flicker in dimmed images through pastel waves, while she sang a duet with Dan Dailey about sailors, mermaids and her home in far Atlantis.

"And now," said Martin, turning with quiet authority to Watt, who was regarding him with a baffled expression, "I want a word with you."

"I can't discuss your contract till Raoul gets back," Watt said quickly.

"Nonsense," Martin said in a firm voice. "Why should St. Cyr dictate your decisions? Without you, he couldn't turn out a box-office success if he had to. No, be quiet, Erika. I'm handling this, my pretty creature."

Watt rose to his feet. "Sorry, I can't discuss it," he said. "St. Cyr pictures make money, and you're an inexperien—"

"That's why I see the true situation so clearly," Martin said. "The trouble with you is you draw a line between artistic genius and financial genius. To you, it's merely routine when you work with the plastic medium of human minds, shaping them into an Ideal Audience. You are an ecological genius, Tolliver Watt! The true artist controls his environment, and gradually you, with a master's consummate skill, shape that great mass of living, breathing humanity into a perfect audience...."

"Sorry," Watt said, but not, bruskly. "I really have no time—ah—"

"Your genius has gone long enough unrecognized," Martin said hastily, letting admiration ring in his golden voice. "You assume that St. Cyr is your equal. You give him your own credit titles. Yet in your own mind you must have known that half the credit for his pictures is yours. Was Phidias non-commercial? Was Michaelangelo? Commercialism is simply a label for functionalism, and all great artists produce functional art. The trivial details of Rubens' masterpieces were filled in by assistants, were they not? But Rubens got the credit, not his hirelings. The proof of the pudding's obvious. Why?" Cunningly gauging his listener, Martin here broke off.

"Why?" Watt asked.

"Sit down," Martin urged. "I'll tell you why. St. Cyr's pictures make money, but you're responsible for their molding into the ideal form, impressing your character-matrix upon everything and everyone at Summit Studios...."

*

Slowly Watt sank into his chair. About his ears the hypnotic bursts of Disraelian rhodomontade thundered compellingly. For Martin had the man hooked. With unerring aim he had at the first try discovered Watt's weakness—the uncomfortable feeling in a professionally arty town that money-making is a basically contemptible business. Disraeli had handled tougher problems in his day. He had swayed Parliaments.

Watt swayed, tottered—and fell. It took about ten minutes, all in all. By the end of that time, dizzy with eloquent praise of his economic ability, Watt had realized that while St. Cyr might be an artistic genius, he had no business interfering in the plans of an economic genius. Nobody told Watt what to do when economics were concerned.

"You have the broad vision that can balance all possibilities and show the right path with perfect clarity," Martin said glibly. "Very well. You wish Eden. You feel—do you not?—that I am unsuitable material. Only geniuses can change their plans with instantaneous speed.... When will my contract release be ready?"

"What?" said Watt, in a swimming, glorious daze. "Oh. Of course. Hm-m. Your contract release. Well, now—"

"St. Cyr would stubbornly cling to past errors until Summit goes broke," Martin pointed out. "Only a genius like Tolliver Watt strikes when the iron is hot, when he sees a chance to exchange failure for success, a Martin for an Eden."

"Hm-m," Watt said. "Yes. Very well, then." His long face grew shrewd. "Very, well, you get your release—*after* I've signed Eden."

"There you put your finger on the heart of the matter," Martin approved, after a very brief moment of somewhat dashed thought. "Miss Eden is still undecided. If you left the transaction to somebody like St. Cyr, say, it would be botched. Erika, you have your car here? How quickly could you drive Tolliver Watt to Laguna? He's the only person with the skill to handle this situation."

"What situa—oh, yes. Of course, Nick. We could start right away."

"But—" Watt said.

The Disraeli-matrix swept on into oratorical periods that made the walls ring. The golden tongue played arpeggios with logic.

"I see," the dazed Watt murmured, allowing himself to be shepherded toward the door. "Yes, yes, of course. Then—suppose you drop over to my place tonight, Martin. After I get the Eden signature, I'll have your release prepared. Hm-m. Functional genius...." His voice fell to a low, crooning mutter, and he moved quietly out of the door.

Martin laid a hand on Erika's arm as she followed him.

"Wait a second," he said. "Keep him away from the studio until we get the release. St. Cyr can still out-shout me any time. But he's hooked. We—"

"Nick," Erika said, looking searchingly into his face. "What's happened?"

"Tell you tonight," Martin said hastily, hearing a distant bellow that might be the voice of St. Cyr approaching. "When I have time I'm going to sweep you off your feet. Did you know that I've worshipped you from afar all my life? But right now, get Watt out of the way. Hurry!"

Erika cast a glance of amazed bewilderment at him as he thrust her out of the door. Martin thought there was a certain element of pleasure in the surprise.

*

"Where is Tolliver?" The loud, annoyed roar of St. Cyr made Martin wince. The director was displeased, it appeared, because only in Costumes could a pair of trousers be found large enough to fit him. He took it as a personal affront. "What have you done with Tolliver?" he bellowed.

"Louder, please," Martin said insolently. "I can't hear you."

"DeeDee," St. Cyr shouted, whirling toward the lovely star, who hadn't stirred from her rapturous admiration of DeeDee in technicolor overhead. "Where is Tolliver?"

Martin started. He had quite forgotten DeeDee.

"You don't know, do you, DeeDee?" he prompted quickly.

"Shut up," St. Cyr snapped. "Answer me, you—" He added a brisk polysyllable in Mixo-Lydian, with the desired effect. DeeDee wrinkled her flawless brow.

"Tolliver went away, I think. I've got it mixed up with the picture. He went home to meet Nick Martin, didn't he?"

"See?" Martin interrupted, relieved. "No use expecting DeeDee to—"

"But Martin is *here*!" St. Cyr shouted. "Think, think!"

"Was the contract release in the rushes?" DeeDee asked vaguely.

"A contract release?" St. Cyr roared. "What is this? Never will I permit it, never, never, never! DeeDee, answer me—where has Watt gone?"

"He went somewhere with that agent," DeeDee said. "Or was that in the rushes too?"

"But where, where, where?"

"They went to Atlantis," DeeDee announced with an air of faint triumph.

"No!" shouted St. Cyr. "That was the *picture*! The mermaid came from Atlantis, not Watt!"

"Tolliver didn't say he was coming from Atlantis," DeeDee murmured, unruffled. "He said he was going to Atlantis. Then he was going to meet Nick Martin at his house tonight and give him his contract release."

"When?" St. Cyr demanded furiously. "Think, DeeDee? What time did—"

"DeeDee," Martin said, stepping forward with suave confidence, "you can't remember a thing, can you?" But DeeDee was too subnormal to react even to a Disraeli-matrix. She merely smiled placidly at him.

"Out of my way, you writer!" roared St. Cyr, advancing upon Martin. "You will get no contract release! You do not waste St. Cyr's time and get away with it! This I will not endure. I fix you as I fixed Ed Cassidy!"

Martin drew himself up and froze St. Cyr with an insolent smile. His hand toyed with an imaginary monocle. Golden periods were hanging at the end of his tongue. There only remained to hypnotize

St. Cyr as he had hypnotized Watt. He drew a deep breath to unlease the floods of his eloquence—

And St. Cyr, also too subhuman to be impressed by urbanity, hit Martin a clout on the jaw.

It could never have happened in the British Parliament.

III

When the robot walked into Martin's office that evening, he, or it, went directly to the desk, unscrewed the bulb from the lamp, pressed the switch, and stuck his finger into the socket. There was a crackling flash. ENIAC withdrew his finger and shook his metallic head violently.

"I needed that," he sighed. "I've been on the go all day, by the Kaldekooz time-scale. Paleolithic, Neolithic, Technological—I don't even know what time it is. Well, how's your ecological adjustment getting on?"

Martin rubbed his chin thoughtfully.

"Badly," he said. "Tell me, did Disraeli, as Prime Minister, ever have any dealings with a country called Mixo-Lydia?"

"I have no idea," said the robot. "Why do you ask?"

"Because my environment hauled back and took a poke at my jaw," Martin said shortly.

"Then you provoked it," ENIAC countered. "A crisis—a situation of stress—always brings a man's dominant trait to the fore, and Disraeli was dominantly courageous. Under stress, his courage became insolence. But he was intelligent enough to arrange his environment so insolence would be countered on the semantic level. Mixo-Lydia, eh? I place it vaguely, some billions of years ago, when it was inhabited by giant white apes. Or—oh, now I remember. It's an encysted medieval survival, isn't it?"

Martin nodded.

"So is this movie studio," the robot said. "Your trouble is that you've run up against somebody who's got a better optimum ecological adjustment than you have. That's it. This studio environment is just emerging from medievalism, so it can easily slip back into that plenum when an optimum medievalist exerts pressure. Such types caused the Dark Ages. Well, you'd better change your environment to a neo-technological one, where the Disraeli matrix can be successfully pro-survival. In your era, only a few archaic social-encystments like this studio are feudalistic, so go somewhere else. It takes a feudalist to match a feudalist."

"But I can't go somewhere else," Martin complained. "Not without my contract release. I was supposed to pick it up tonight, but St. Cyr found out what was happening, and he'll throw a monkey-wrench in the works if he has to knock me out again to do it. I'm due at Watt's place now, but St. Cyr's already there—"

"Spare me the trivia," the robot said, raising his hand. "As for this St. Cyr, if he's a medieval character-type, obviously he'll knuckle under only to a stronger man of his own kind."

"How would Disraeli have handled this?" Martin demanded.

"Disraeli would never have got into such a situation in the first place," the robot said unhelpfully. "The ecologizer can give you the ideal ecological differential, but only for your own type, because otherwise it wouldn't be your optimum. Disraeli would have been a failure in Russia in Ivan's time."

"Would you mind clarifying that?" Martin asked thoughtfully.

"Certainly," the robot said with great rapidity. "It all depends on the threshold-response-time of the memory-circuits in the brain, if you assume the identity of the basic chromosome-pattern. The strength of neuronic activation varies in inverse proportion to the quantative memory factor. Only actual experience could give you Disraeli's memories, but your reactivity-thresholds have been altered until perception and emotional-indices approximate the Disraeli ratio."

"Oh," Martin said. "But how would *you*, say, assert yourself against a medieval steam-shovel?"

"By plugging my demountable brain into a larger steam-shovel," ENIAC told him.

*

Martin seemed pensive. His hand rose, adjusting an invisible monocle, while a look of perceptive imagination suddenly crossed his face.

"You mentioned Russia in Ivan's time," he said. "Which Ivan would that be? Not, by any chance—?"

"Ivan the Fourth. Very well adjusted to his environment he was, too. However, enough of this chit-chat. Obviously you'll be one of the failures in our experiment, but our aim is to strike an average, so if you'll put the ecologizer on your—"

"That was Ivan the Terrible, wasn't it?" Martin interrupted. "Look here, could you impress the character-matrix of Ivan the Terrible on my brain?"

"That wouldn't help you a bit," the robot said. "Besides, it's not the purpose of the experiment. Now—"

"One moment. Disraeli can't cope with a medievalist like St. Cyr on his own level, but if I had Ivan the Terrible's reactive thresholds, I'll bet I could throw a bluff that might do the trick. Even though St. Cyr's bigger than I am, he's got a veneer of civilization ... now wait. He trades on that. He's always dealt with people who are too civilized to use his own methods. The trick would be to call his bluff. And Ivan's the man who could do it."

"But you don't understand."

"Didn't everybody in Russia tremble with fear at Ivan's name?"

"Yes, in—"

"Very well, then," Martin said triumphantly. "You're going to impress the character-matrix, of Ivan the Terrible on my mind, and then I'm going to put the bite on St. Cyr, the way Ivan would have done it. Disraeli's simply too civilized. Size is a factor, but character's more important. I don't look like Disraeli, but people have been reacting to me as though I were George Arliss down to the spit-curl.

HENRY KUTTNER AND C. L. MOORE

A good big man can always lick a good little man. But St. Cyr's never been up against a really uncivilized little man—one who'd gladly rip out an enemy's heart with his bare hands." Martin nodded briskly. "St. Cyr will back down—I've found that out. But it would take somebody like Ivan to make him stay all the way down."

"If you think I'm going to impress Ivan's matrix on you, you're wrong," the robot said.

"You couldn't be talked into it?"

"I," said ENIAC, "am a robot, semantically adjusted. Of course you couldn't talk me into it."

Perhaps not, Martin reflected, but Disraeli—hm-m. "Man is a machine." Why, Disraeli was the one person in the world ideally fitted for robot-coercion. To him, men *were* machines—and what was ENIAC?

"Let's talk this over—" Martin began, absently pushing the desk-lamp toward the robot. And then the golden tongue that had swayed empires was loosed....

"You're not going to like this," the robot said dazedly, sometime later. "Ivan won't do at ... oh, you've got me all confused. You'll have to eyeprint a—" He began to pull out of his sack the helmet and the quarter-mile of red ribbon.

"To tie up my bonny grey brain," Martin said, drunk with his own rhetoric. "Put it on my head. That's right. Ivan the Terrible, remember. I'll fix St. Cyr's Mixo-Lydian wagon."

"Differential depends on environment as much as on heredity," the robot muttered, clapping the helmet on Martin's head. "Though naturally Ivan wouldn't have had the Tsardom environment without his particular heredity, involving Helena Glinska—there!" He removed the helmet.

"But nothing's happening," Martin said. "I don't feel any different."

"It'll take a few moments. This isn't your basic character-pattern, remember, as Disraeli's was. Enjoy yourself while you can. You'll get the Ivan-effect soon enough." He shouldered the sack and headed uncertainly for the door.

"Wait," Martin said uneasily. "Are you sure—"

"Be quiet. I forgot something—some formality—now I'm all confused. Well, I'll think of it later, or earlier, as the case may be. I'll see you in twelve hours—I hope."

The robot departed. Martin shook his head tentatively from side to side. Then he got up and followed ENIAC to the door. But there was no sign of the robot, except for a diminishing whirlwind of dust in the middle of the corridor.

Something began to happen in Martin's brain....

Behind him, the telephone rang.

Martin heard himself gasp with pure terror. With a sudden, impossible, terrifying, absolute certainty he *knew* who was telephoning.

Assassins!

*

"Yes, Mr. Martin," said Tolliver Watt's butler to the telephone. "Miss Ashby is here. She is with Mr. Watt and Mr. St. Cyr at the moment, but I will give her your message. You are detained. And she is to call for you—where?"

"The broom-closet on the second floor of the Writers' Building," Martin said in a quavering voice. "It's the only one near a telephone with a long enough cord so I could take the phone in here with me. But I'm not at all certain that I'm safe. I don't like the looks of that broom on my left."

"Sir?"

"Are you *sure* you're Tolliver Watt's butler?" Martin demanded nervously.

"Quite sure, Mr.—eh—Mr. Martin."

"I *am* Mr. Martin," cried Martin with terrified defiance. "By all the laws of God and man, Mr. Martin I am and Mr. Martin I will remain,

38

in spite of all attempts by rebellious dogs to depose me from my rightful place."

"Yes, sir. The broom-closet, you say, sir?"

"The broom-closet. Immediately. But swear not to tell another soul, no matter how much you're threatened. I'll protect you."

"Very well, sir. Is that all?"

"Yes. Tell Miss Ashby to hurry. Hang up now. The line may be tapped. I have enemies."

There was a click. Martin replaced his own receiver and furtively surveyed the broom-closet. He told himself that this was ridiculous. There was nothing to be afraid of, was there? True, the broom-closet's narrow walls were closing in upon him alarmingly, while the ceiling descended....

Panic-stricken, Martin emerged from the closet, took a long breath, and threw back his shoulders. "N-not a thing to be afraid of," he said. "Who's afraid?" Whistling, he began to stroll down the hall toward the staircase, but midway agoraphobia overcame him, and his nerve broke.

He ducked into his own office and sweated quietly in the dark until he had mustered up enough courage to turn on a lamp.

The Encyclopedia Britannica, in its glass-fronted cabinet, caught his eye. With noiseless haste, Martin secured *ITALY* to *LORD* and opened the volume at his desk. Something, obviously, was very, very wrong. The robot had said that Martin wasn't going to like being Ivan the Terrible, come to think of it. But was Martin wearing Ivan's character-matrix? Perhaps he'd got somebody else's matrix by mistake—that of some arrant coward. Or maybe the Mad Tsar of Russia had really been called Ivan the Terrified. Martin flipped the rustling pages nervously. Ivan, Ivan—here it was.

Son of Helena Glinska ... married Anastasia Zakharina-Koshkina ... private life unspeakably abominable ... memory astonishing, energy indefatigable, ungovernable fury—great natural ability, political foresight, anticipated the ideals of Peter the Great—Martin shook his head.

Then he caught his breath at the next line.

Ivan had lived in an atmosphere of apprehension, imagining that every man's hand was against him.

"Just like me," Martin murmured. "But—but there was more to Ivan than just cowardice. I don't understand."

"Differential," the robot had said, "depends on environment as much as on heredity. Though naturally Ivan wouldn't have had the Tsardom environment without his particular heredity."

Martin sucked in his breath sharply. Environment does make a difference. No doubt Ivan IV had been a fearful coward, but heredity plus environment had given Ivan the one great weapon that had enabled him to keep his cowardice a recessive trait.

Ivan the Terrible had been Tsar of all the Russias.

Give a coward a gun, and, while he doesn't stop being a coward, it won't show in the same way. He may act like a violent, aggressive tyrant instead. That, of course, was why Ivan had been ecologically successful—in his specialized environment. He'd never run up against many stresses that brought his dominant trait to the fore. Like Disraeli, he had been able to control his environment so that such stresses were practically eliminated.

Martin turned green.

Then he remembered Erika. Could he get Erika to keep St. Cyr busy, somehow, while he got his contract release from Watt? As long as he could avoid crises, he could keep his nerve from crumbling, but—*there were assassins everywhere!*

Erika was on her way to the lot by now. Martin swallowed.

He would meet her outside the studio. The broom-closet wasn't safe. He could be trapped there like a rat—

"Nonsense," Martin told himself with shivering firmness. "This isn't me. All I have to do is get a g-grip on m-myself. Come, now. Buck up. *Toujours l'audace!*"

But he went out of his office and downstairs very softly and cautiously. After all, one never knew. And when every man's hand was against one....

Quaking, the character-matrix of Ivan the Terrible stole toward a studio gate.

*

The taxi drove rapidly toward Bel-Air.

"But what were you doing up that tree?" Erika demanded.

Martin shook violently.

"A werewolf," he chattered. "And a vampire and a ghoul and—I *saw* them, I tell you. There I was at the studio gate, and they all came at me in a mob."

"But they were just coming back from dinner," Erika said. "You know Summit's doing night shooting on *Abbott and Costello Meet Everybody.* Karloff wouldn't hurt a fly."

"I kept telling myself that," Martin said dully, "but I was out of my mind with guilt and fear. You see, I'm an abominable monster. But it's not my fault. It's environmental. I grew up in brutal and degrading conditions—oh, look!" He pointed toward a traffic cop ahead. "The police! Traitors even in the palace guards!"

"Lady, is that guy nuts?" the cabbie demanded.

"Mad or sane, I am Nicholas Martin," Martin announced, with an abrupt volte face. He tried to stand up commandingly, bumped his head, screamed "*Assassins!*" and burrowed into a corner of the seat, panting horribly.

Erika gave him a thoughtful, worried look.

"Nick," she said, "How much have you had to drink? What's wrong?"

Martin shut his eyes and lay back against the cushions.

"Let me have a few minutes, Erika," he pleaded. "I'll be all right as soon as I recover from stress. It's only when I'm under stress that Ivan—"

"You can accept your contract release from Watt, can't you? Surely you'll be able to manage that."

41

"Of course," Martin said with feeble bravery. He thought it over and reconsidered. "If I can hold your hand," he suggested, taking no chances.

This disgusted Erika so much that for two miles there was no more conversation within the cab.

Erika had been thinking her own thoughts.

"You've certainly changed since this morning," she observed. "Threatening to make love to me, of all things. As if I'd stand for it. I'd like to see you try." There was a pause. Erika slid her eyes sidewise toward Martin. "I said I'd like to see you try," she repeated.

"Oh, you would, would you?" Martin said with hollow valor. He paused. Oddly enough his tongue, hitherto frozen stiff on one particular subject in Erika's presence, was now thoroughly loosened. Martin wasted no time on theory. Seizing his chance before a new stress might unexpectedly arise, he instantly poured out his heart to Erika, who visibly softened.

"But why didn't you ever say so before?" she asked.

"I can't imagine," Martin said. "Then you'll marry me?"

"But why were you acting so—"

"Will you marry me?"

"Yes," Erika said, and there was a pause. Martin moistened his lips, discovering that somehow he and Erika had moved close together. He was about to seal the bargain in the customary manner when a sudden thought struck him and made him draw back with a little start.

Erika opened her eyes.

"Ah—" said Martin. "Um. I just happened to remember. There's a bad flu epidemic in Chicago. Epidemics spread like wildfire, you know. Why, it could be in Hollywood by now—especially with the prevailing westerly winds."

"I'm damned if I'm going to be proposed to and not kissed," Erika said in a somewhat irritated tone. "You kiss me!"

"But I might give you bubonic plague," Martin said nervously.

"Kissing spreads germs. It's a well-known fact."

"Nick!"

"Well—I don't know—when did you last have a cold?"

Erika pulled away from him and went to sit in the other corner.

"Ah," Martin said, after a long silence. "Erika?"

"Don't talk to me, you miserable man," Erika said. "You monster, you."

"I can't help it," Martin cried wildly. "I'll be a coward for twelve hours. It's not my fault. After eight tomorrow morning I'll—I'll walk into a lion-cage if you want, but tonight I'm as yellow as Ivan the Terrible! At least let me tell you what's been happening."

Erika said nothing. Martin instantly plunged into his long and improbable tale.

"I don't believe a word of it," Erika said, when he had finished. She shook her head sharply. "Just the same, I'm still your agent, and your career's still my responsibility. The first and only thing we have to do is get your contract release from Tolliver Watt. And that's *all* we're going to consider right now, do you hear?"

"But St. Cyr—"

"I'll do all the talking. You won't have to say a word. If St. Cyr tries to bully you, I'll handle him. But you've got to be there with me, or St. Cyr will make that an excuse to postpone things again. I know him."

"Now I'm under stress again," Martin said wildly. "I can't stand it. *I'm* not the Tsar of Russia."

"Lady," said the cab-driver, looking back, "if I was you, I'd sure as hell break off that engagement."

"Heads will roll for this," Martin said ominously.

*

"By mutual consent, agree to terminate ... yes," Watt said, affixing his name to the legal paper that lay before him on the desk. "That does it. But where in the world is that fellow Martin? He came in with you, I'm certain."

"Did he?" Erika asked, rather wildly. She too, was wondering how Martin had managed to vanish so miraculously from her side. Perhaps he had crept with lightning rapidity under the carpet. She forced her mind from the thought and reached for the contract release Watt was folding.

"Wait," St. Cyr said, his lower lip jutting. "What about a clause giving us an option on Martin's next play?"

Watt paused, and the director instantly struck home.

"Whatever it may be, I can turn it into a vehicle for DeeDee, eh, DeeDee?" He lifted a sausage finger at the lovely star, who nodded obediently.

"It's going to have an all-male cast," Erika said hastily. "And we're discussing contract releases, not options."

"He would give me an option if I had him here," St. Cyr growled, torturing his cigar horribly. "Why does everything conspire against an artist?" He waved a vast, hairy fist in the air. "Now I must break in a new writer, which is a great waste. Within a fortnight Martin would have been a St. Cyr writer. In fact, it is still possible."

"I'm afraid not, Raoul," Watt said resignedly. "You really shouldn't have hit Martin at the studio today."

"But—but he would not dare charge me with assault. In Mixo-Lydia—"

"Why, hello, Nick," DeeDee said, with a bright smile. "What are you hiding behind those curtains for?"

Every eye was turned toward the window draperies, just in time to see the white, terrified face of Nicholas Martin flip out of sight like a scared chipmunk's. Erika, her heart dropping, said hastily, "Oh, that isn't Nick. It doesn't look a bit like him. You made a mistake, DeeDee."

"Did I?" DeeDee asked, perfectly willing to agree.

"Certainly," Erika said, reaching for the contract release in Watt's hand. "Now if you'll just let me have this, I'll—"

"Stop!" cried St. Cyr in a bull's bellow. Head sunk between his heavy shoulders, he lumbered to the window and jerked the curtains aside.

"Ha!" the director said in a sinister voice. "Martin."

"It's a lie," Martin said feebly, making a desperate attempt to conceal his stress-triggered panic. "I've abdicated."

St. Cyr, who had stepped back a pace, was studying Martin carefully. Slowly the cigar in his mouth began to tilt upwards. An unpleasant grin widened the director's mouth.

He shook a finger under Martin's quivering nostrils.

"You!" he said. "Tonight it is a different tune, eh? Today you were drunk. Now I see it all. Valorous with pots, like they say."

"Nonsense," Martin said, rallying his courage by a glance at Erika. "Who say? Nobody but you would say a thing like that. Now what's this all about?"

"What were you doing behind that curtain?" Watt asked.

"*I* wasn't behind the curtain," Martin said, with great bravado. "*You* were. All of you. I was in front of the curtain. Can I help it if the whole lot of you conceal yourselves behind curtains in a library, like—like conspirators?" The word was unfortunately chosen. A panicky light flashed into Martin's eyes. "Yes, conspirators," he went on nervously. "You think I don't know, eh? Well, I do. You're all assassins, plotting and planning. So this is your headquarters, is it? All night your hired dogs have been at my heels, driving me like a wounded caribou to—"

"We've got to be going," Erika said desperately. "There's just time to catch the next carib—the next plane east." She reached for the contract release, but Watt suddenly put it in his pocket. He turned his chair toward Martin.

"Will you give us an option on your next play?" he demanded.

"Of course he will give us an option!" St. Cyr said, studying Martin's air of bravado with an experienced eye. "Also, there is to be no question of a charge of assault, for, if there is I will beat you. So it is in Mixo-Lydia. In fact, you do not even want a release from your contract, Martin. It is all a mistake. I will turn you into a St. Cyr writer, and all will be well. So. Now you will ask Tolliver to tear up that release, will you not—*ha*?"

"Of course you won't, Nick," Erika cried. "Say so!"

*

There was a pregnant silence. Watt watched with sharp interest. So did the unhappy Erika, torn between her responsibility as Martin's agent and her disgust at the man's abject cowardice. DeeDee watched too, her eyes very wide and a cheerful smile upon her handsome face. But the battle was obviously between Martin and Raoul St. Cyr.

Martin drew himself up desperately. Now or never he must force himself to be truly Terrible. Already he had a troubled expression, just like Ivan. He strove to look sinister too. An enigmatic smile played around his lips. For an instant he resembled the Mad Tsar of Russia, except, of course, that he was clean-shaven. With contemptuous, regal power Martin stared down the Mixo-Lydian.

"You will tear up that release and sign an agreement giving us option on your next play too, ha?" St. Cyr said—but a trifle uncertainly.

"I'll do as I please," Martin told him. "How would you like to be eaten alive by dogs?"

"I don't know, Raoul," Watt said. "Let's try to get this settled even if—"

"Do you want me to go over to Metro and take DeeDee with me?" St. Cyr cried, turning toward Watt. "He *will* sign!" And, reaching into an inner pocket for a pen, the burly director swung back toward Martin.

"*Assassin!*" cried Martin, misinterpreting the gesture.

A gloating smile appeared on St. Cyr's revolting features.

"Now we have him, Tolliver," he said, with heavy triumph, and these ominous words added the final stress to Martin's overwhelming burden. With a mad cry he rushed past St. Cyr, wrenched open a door, and fled.

From behind him came Erika's Valkyrie voice.

"Leave him alone! Haven't you done enough already? Now I'm going to get that contract release from you before I leave this room, Tolliver Watt, and I warn you, St. Cyr, if you—"

But by then Martin was five rooms away, and the voice faded. He darted on, hopelessly trying to make himself slow down and return to the scene of battle. The pressure was too strong. Terror hurled him down a corridor, into another room, and against a metallic object from which he rebounded, to find himself sitting on the floor looking up at ENIAC Gamma the Ninety-Third.

"Ah, there you are," the robot said. "I've been searching all over space-time for you. You forgot to give me a waiver of responsibility when you talked me into varying the experiment. The Authorities would be in my gears if I didn't bring back an eyeprinted waiver when a subject's scratched by variance."

With a frightened glance behind him, Martin rose to his feet.

"What?" he asked confusedly. "Listen, you've got to change me back to myself. Everyone's trying to kill me. You're just in time. I can't wait twelve hours. Change me back to myself, quick!"

"Oh, I'm through with you," the robot said callously. "You're no longer a suitably unconditioned subject, after that last treatment you insisted on. I should have got the waiver from you then, but you got me all confused with Disraeli's oratory. Now here. Just hold this up to your left eye for twenty seconds." He extended a flat, glittering little metal disk. "It's already sensitized and filled out. It only needs your eyeprint. Affix it, and you'll never see me again."

Martin shrank away.

"But what's going to happen to me?" he quavered, swallowing.

"How should I know? After twelve hours, the treatment will wear off, and you'll be yourself again. Hold this up to your eye, now."

"I will if you'll change me back to myself," Martin haggled.

"I can't. It's against the rules. One variance is bad enough, even with a filed waiver, but two? Oh, no. Hold this up to your left eye—"

"No," Martin said with feeble firmness. "I won't."

ENIAC studied him.

"Yes, you will," the robot said finally, "or I'll go boo at you."

Martin paled slightly, but he shook his head in desperate determination.

"No," he said doggedly. "Unless I get rid of Ivan's matrix right now, Erika will never marry me and I'll never get my contract release from Watt. All you have to do is put that helmet on my head and change me back to myself. Is that too much to ask?"

"Certainly, of a robot," ENIAC said stiffly. "No more shilly-shallying. It's lucky you are wearing the Ivan-matrix, so I can impose my will on you. Put your eyeprint on this. Instantly!"

Martin rushed behind the couch and hid. The robot advanced menacingly. And at that moment, pushed to the last ditch, Martin suddenly remembered something.

He faced the robot.

*

"Wait," he said. "You don't understand. I can't eyeprint that thing. It won't work on me. Don't you realize that? It's supposed to take the eyeprint—"

"—of the rod-and-cone pattern of the retina," the robot said. "So—"

"So how can it do that unless I can keep my eye open for twenty seconds? My perceptive reaction-thresholds are Ivan's aren't they? I can't control the reflex of blinking. I've got a coward's synapses. And they'd force me to shut my eyes tight the second that gimmick got too close to them."

"Hold them open," the robot suggested. "With your fingers."

"My fingers have reflexes too," Martin argued, moving toward a sideboard. "There's only one answer. I've got to get drunk. If I'm half stupefied with liquor, my reflexes will be so slow I won't be able to shut my eyes. And don't try to use force, either. If I dropped dead with fear, how could you get my eyeprint then?"

"Very easily," the robot said. "I'd pry open your lids—"

Martin hastily reached for a bottle on the sideboard, and a glass. But his hand swerved aside and gripped, instead, a siphon of soda water.

"—only," ENIAC went on, "the forgery might be detected."

Martin fizzled the glass full of soda and took a long drink.

"I won't be long getting drunk," he said, his voice thickening. "In fact, it's beginning to work already. See? I'm coöperating."

The robot hesitated.

"Well, hurry up about it," he said. and sat down.

Martin, about to take another drink, suddenly paused, staring at ENIAC. Then, with a sharply indrawn breath, he lowered the glass.

"What's the matter now?" the robot asked. "Drink your—what is it?"

"It's whiskey," Martin told the inexperienced automaton, "but now I see it all. You've put poison in it. So that's your plan, is it? Well, I won't touch another drop, and now you'll never get my eyeprint. I'm no fool."

"Cog Almighty," the robot said, rising. "You poured that drink yourself. How could I have poisoned it? Drink!"

"I won't," Martin said, with a coward's stubbornness, fighting back the growing suspicion that the drink might really be toxic.

"You swallow that drink," ENIAC commanded, his voice beginning to quiver slightly. "It's perfectly harmless."

"Then prove it!" Martin said cunningly. "Would you be willing to switch glasses? Would you drink this poisoned brew yourself?"

"How do you expect me to drink?" the robot demanded. "I—" He paused. "All right, hand me the glass," he said. "I'll take a sip. Then you've got to drink the rest of it."

"Aha!" Martin said. "You betrayed yourself that time. You're a robot. You can't drink, remember? Not the same way that I can, anyhow. Now I've got you trapped, you assassin. *There's* your brew." He pointed to a floor-lamp. "Do you dare to drink with me now, in your electrical fashion, or do you admit you are trying to poison me? Wait a minute, what am I saying? That wouldn't prove a—"

"Of course it would," the robot said hastily. "You're perfectly right, and it's very cunning of you. We'll drink together, and that will prove your whiskey's harmless—so you'll keep on drinking till your reflexes slow down, see?"

"Well," Martin began uncertainly, but the unscrupulous robot unscrewed a bulb from the floor lamp, pulled the switch, and inserted his finger into the empty socket, which caused a crackling flash. "There," the robot said. "It isn't poisoned, see?"

"You're not swallowing it," Martin said suspiciously. "You're holding it in your mouth—I mean your finger."

ENIAC again probed the socket.

"Well, all right, perhaps," Martin said, in a doubtful fashion. "But I'm not going to risk your slipping a powder in my liquor, you traitor. You're going to keep up with me, drink for drink, until I can eyeprint that gimmick of yours—or else I stop drinking. But does sticking your finger in that lamp really prove my liquor isn't poisoned? I can't quite—"

"Of course it does," the robot said quickly. "I'll prove it. I'll do it again ... $f(t)$. Powerful DC, isn't it? Certainly it proves it. Keep drinking, now."

*

His gaze watchfully on the robot, Martin lifted his glass of club soda.

"F ff ff $f(t)$!" cried the robot, some time later, sketching a singularly loose smile on its metallic face.

"Best fermented mammoth's milk I ever tasted," Martin agreed, lifting his tenth glass of soda-water. He felt slightly queasy and wondered if he might be drowning.

"Mammoth's milk?" asked ENIAC thickly. "What year is this?"

Martin drew a long breath. Ivan's capacious memory had served him very well so far. Voltage, he recalled, increased the frequency of the robot's thought-patterns and disorganized ENIAC's memory—which was being proved before his eyes. But the crux of his plan was yet to come....

"The year of the great Hairy One, of course," Martin said briskly. "Don't you remember?"

"Then you—" ENIAC strove to focus upon his drinking-companion. "You must be Mammoth-Slayer."

"That's it!" Martin cried. "Have another jolt. What about giving me the treatment now?"

"What treatment?"

Martin looked impatient. "You said you were going to impose the character-matrix of Mammoth-Slayer on my mind. You said *that* would insure my optimum ecological adjustment in this temporal phase, and nothing else would."

"Did I? But you're not Mammoth-Slayer," ENIAC said confusedly. "Mammoth-Slayer was the son of the Great Hairy One. What's your mother's name?"

"The Great Hairy One," Martin replied, at which the robot grated its hand across its gleaming forehead.

"Have one more jolt," Martin suggested. "Now take out the ecologizer and put it on my head."

"Like this?" ENIAC asked, obeying. "I keep feeling I've forgotten something important. $F(t)$."

Martin adjusted the crystal helmet on his skull. "Now," he commanded. "Give me the character-matrix of Mammoth-Slayer, son of the Great Hairy One."

"Well—all right," ENIAC said dizzily. The red ribbons swirled. There was a flash from the helmet. "There," the robot said. "It's done. It may take a few minutes to begin functioning, but then for twelve hours you'll—wait! Where are you going?"

But Martin had already departed.

The robot stuffed the helmet and the quarter-mile of red ribbon back for the last time. He lurched to the floor-lamp, muttering

51

something about one for the road. Afterward, the room lay empty. A fading murmur said, "$F(t)$."

*

"Nick!" Erika gasped, staring at the figure in the doorway. "Don't stand like that! You frighten me!"

Everyone in the room looked up abruptly at her cry, and so were just in time to see a horrifying change take place in Martin's shape. It was an illusion, of course, but an alarming one. His knees slowly bent until he was half-crouching, his shoulders slumped as though bowed by the weight of enormous back and shoulder muscles, and his arms swung forward until their knuckles hung perilously near the floor.

Nicholas Martin had at last achieved a personality whose ecological norm would put him on a level with Raoul St. Cyr.

"Nick!" Erika quavered.

Slowly Martin's jaw protruded till his lower teeth were hideously visible. Gradually his eyelids dropped until he was peering up out of tiny, wicked sockets. Then, slowly, a perfectly shocking grin broadened Mr. Martin's mouth.

"Erika," he said throatily. "Mine!"

And with that, he shambled forward, seized the horrified girl in his arms, and bit her on the ear.

"Oh, Nick," Erika murmured, closing her eyes. "Why didn't you ever—no, no, *no*! Nick! Stop it! The contract release. We've got to—Nick, what are you doing?" She snatched at Martin's departing form, but too late.

For all his ungainly and unpleasant gait, Martin covered ground fast. Almost instantly he was clambering over Watt's desk as the most direct route to that startled tycoon. DeeDee looked on, a little surprised. St. Cyr lunged forward.

"In Mixo-Lydia—" he began. "Ha! So!" He picked up Martin and threw him across the room.

"Oh, you beast," Erika cried, and flung herself upon the director,

52

beating at his brawny chest. On second thought, she used her shoes on his shins with more effect. St. Cyr, no gentleman, turned her around, pinioned her arms behind her, and glanced up at Watt's alarmed cry.

"Martin! What are you doing?"

There was reason for his inquiry. Apparently unhurt by St. Cyr's toss, Martin had hit the floor, rolled over and over like a ball, knocked down a floor-lamp with a crash, and uncurled, with an unpleasant expression on his face. He rose crouching, bandy-legged, his arms swinging low, a snarl curling his lips.

"You take my mate?" the pithecanthropic Mr. Martin inquired throatily, rapidly losing all touch with the twentieth century. It was a rhetorical question. He picked up the lamp-standard—he did not have to bend to do it—tore off the silk shade as he would have peeled foliage from a tree-limb, and balanced the weapon in his hand. Then he moved forward, carrying the lamp-standard like a spear.

"I," said Martin, "kill."

He then endeavored, with the most admirable single-heartedness, to carry out his expressed intention. The first thrust of the blunt, improvised spear rammed into St. Cyr's solar plexus and drove him back against the wall with a booming thud. This seemed to be what Martin wanted. Keeping one end of his spear pressed into the director's belly, he crouched lower, dug his toes into the rug, and did his very best to drill a hole in St. Cyr.

"Stop it!" cried Watt, flinging himself into the conflict. Ancient reflexes took over. Martin's arm shot out. Watt shot off in the opposite direction.

The lamp broke.

Martin looked pensively at the pieces, tentatively began to bite one, changed his mind, and looked at St. Cyr instead. The gasping director, mouthing threats, curses and objections, drew himself up, and shook a huge fist at Martin.

"I," he announced, "shall kill you with my bare hands. Then I go over to MGM with DeeDee. In Mixo-Lydia—"

Martin lifted his own fists toward his face. He regarded them. He unclenched them slowly, while a terrible grin spread across his face. And then, with every tooth showing, and with the hungry gleam of a mad tiger in his tiny little eyes, he lifted his gaze to St. Cyr's throat.

Mammoth-Slayer was not the son of the Great Hairy One for nothing.

*

Martin sprang.

So did St. Cyr—in another direction, screaming with sudden terror. For, after all, he was only a medievalist. The feudal man is far more civilized than the so-called man of Mammoth-Slayer's primordially direct era, and as a man recoils from a small but murderous wildcat, so St. Cyr fled in sudden civilized horror from an attacker who was, literally, afraid of nothing.

He sprang through the window and, shrieking, vanished into the night.

Martin was taken by surprise. When Mammoth-Slayer leaped at an enemy, the enemy leaped at him too, and so Martin's head slammed against the wall with disconcerting force. Dimly he heard diminishing, terrified cries. Laboriously he crawled to his feet and set back against the wall, snarling, quite ready....

"Nick!" Erika's voice called. "Nick, it's me! Stop it! *Stop it!* DeeDee—"

"Ugh?" Martin said thickly, shaking his head. "Kill." He growled softly, blinking through red-rimmed little eyes at the scene around him. It swam back slowly into focus. Erika was struggling with DeeDee near the window.

"You let me go," DeeDee cried. "Where Raoul goes, I go."

"DeeDee!" pleaded a new voice. Martin glanced aside to see Tolliver Watt crumpled in a corner, a crushed lamp-shade half obscuring his face.

With a violent effort Martin straightened up. Walking upright seemed unnatural, somehow, but it helped submerge Mammoth-Slayer's worst instincts. Besides, with St. Cyr gone, stresses were slowly subsiding, so that Mammoth-Slayer's dominant trait was receding from the active foreground.

Martin tested his tongue cautiously, relieved to find he was still capable of human speech.

"Uh," he said. "Arrgh ... ah. Watt."

Watt blinked at him anxiously through the lamp-shade.

"Urgh ... Ur—release," Martin said, with a violent effort. "Contract release. Gimme."

Watt had courage. He crawled to his feet, removing the lamp-shade.

"Contract release!" he snapped. "You madman! Don't you realize what you've done? DeeDee's walking out on me. DeeDee, don't go. We will bring Raoul back—"

"Raoul told me to quit if he quit," DeeDee said stubbornly.

"You don't have to do what St. Cyr tells you," Erika said, hanging onto the struggling star.

"Don't I?" DeeDee asked, astonished. "Yes, I do. I always have."

"DeeDee," Watt said frantically, "I'll give you the finest contract on earth—a ten-year contract—look, here it is." He tore out a well-creased document. "All you have to do is sign, and you can have anything you want. Wouldn't you like that?"

"Oh, yes," DeeDee said. "But Raoul wouldn't like it." She broke free from Erika.

"Martin!" Watt told the playwright frantically, "Get St. Cyr back. Apologize to him. I don't care how, but get him back! If you don't, I—I'll never give you your release."

Martin was observed to slump slightly—perhaps with hopelessness. Then, again, perhaps not.

"I'm sorry," DeeDee said. "I liked working for you, Tolliver. But I have to do what Raoul says, of course." And she moved toward the window.

Martin had slumped further down, till his knuckles quite brushed the rug. His angry little eyes, glowing with baffled rage, were fixed on DeeDee. Slowly his lips peeled back, exposing every tooth in his head.

"You," he said, in an ominous growl.

DeeDee paused, but only briefly.

*

Then the enraged roar of a wild beast reverberated through the room. "*You come back!*" bellowed the infuriated Mammoth-Slayer, and with one agile bound sprang to the window, seized DeeDee and slung her under one arm. Wheeling, he glared jealously at the shrinking Watt and reached for Erika. In a trice he had the struggling forms of both girls captive, one under each arm. His wicked little eyes glanced from one to another. Then, playing no favorites, he bit each quickly on the ear.

"Nick!" Erika cried. "How dare you!"

"Mine," Mammoth-Slayer informed her hoarsely.

"You bet I am," Erika said, "but that works both ways. Put down that hussy you've got under your other arm."

Mammoth-Slayer was observed to eye DeeDee doubtfully.

"Well," Erika said tartly, "make up your mind."

"Both," said the uncivilized playwright. "Yes."

"No!" Erika said.

"Yes," DeeDee breathed in an entirely new tone. Limp as a dishrag, the lovely creature hung from Martin's arm and gazed up at her captor with idolatrous admiration.

"Oh, you hussy," Erika said. "What about St. Cyr?"

"Him," DeeDee said scornfully. "He hasn't got a thing, the sissy. I'll never look at him again." She turned her adoring gaze back to Martin.

56

"Pah," the latter grunted, tossing DeeDee into Watt's lap. "Yours. Keep her." He grinned approvingly at Erika. "Strong she. Better."

Both Watt and DeeDee remained motionless, staring at Martin.

"You," he said, thrusting a finger at DeeDee. "You stay with him. Ha?" He indicated Watt.

DeeDee nodded in slavish adoration.

"You sign contract?"

Nod.

Martin looked significantly into Watt's eyes. He extended his hand.

"The contract release," Erika explained, upside-down. "Give it to him before he pulls your head off."

Slowly Watt pulled the contract release from his pocket and held it out. But Martin was already shambling toward the window. Erika reached back hastily and snatched the document.

"That was a wonderful act," she told Nick, as they reached the street. "Put me down now. We can find a cab some—"

"No act," Martin growled. "Real. Till tomorrow. After that—" He shrugged. "But tonight, Mammoth-Slayer." He attempted to climb a palm tree, changed his mind, and shambled on, carrying the now pensive Erika. But it was not until a police car drove past that Erika screamed....

*

"I'll bail you out tomorrow," Erika told Mammoth-Slayer, struggling between two large patrolmen.

Her words were drowned in an infuriated bellow.

Thereafter events blurred, to solidify again for the irate Mammoth-Slayer only when he was thrown in a cell, where he picked himself up with a threatening roar. "I kill!" he announced, seizing the bars. "*Arrrgh!*"

"Two in one night," said a bored voice, moving away outside. "Both in Bel-Air, too. Think they're hopped up? We couldn't get a coherent story out of either one."

The bars shook. An annoyed voice from one of the bunks said to shut up, and added that there had been already enough trouble from nincompoops without—here it paused, hesitated, and uttered a shrill, sharp, piercing cry.

Silence prevailed, momentarily, in the cell-block as Mammoth-Slayer, son of the Great Hairy One, turned slowly to face Raoul St. Cyr.

www.ingramcontent.com/pod-product-compliance
Lightning Source LLC
Chambersburg PA
CBHW050911120626
46552CB00004B/1518